This book belongs to

_____

This book is dedicated to my children - Mikey, Kobe, and Jojo.
Always follow your passions.

Bruce Lee

By Mary Nhin

Pictures By
Yuliia Zolotova

Some people call me the father of mixed martial arts. Others see me as a movie star. But what some might not know is that I struggled to get there...

When I was younger, I got into a lot of fights.

Unfortunately, I was the one getting beat up. So I begged my mother and father to let me train in martial arts. At first, they resisted. But finally, they gave in due to my persistence.

I trained under Master Yip Man for five years. It was hard but I loved every moment of it.

What shall I learn today, teacher?

Stand in the corner and practice your horse stance.

But I can do that at home. I want to learn how to fight.

You must learn the basics first, Bruce.

Whenever I set my mind on doing something, I could become a diligent student of the task. Like when I decided to learn Cha Cha, I noted 108 different cha cha steps in my journal. Soon after, I won the Hong Kong Cha Cha Championship.

When I took up boxing, I got beat up at first but I didn't give up. I practiced and studied, and eventually won an interschool boxing championship.

As I got older, I was still getting into fights. It got so bad that my parents feared for my life.

Something had to change.

So with $100 in my pocket, I set off for America.

What my father and mother didn't know was that I was soon to face even more hurdles...

When I got to America, I worked at a restaurant but then quickly realized that I could teach martial arts to others. I was thrilled to be doing what I loved.

Soon, I started a martial arts school. While creating my own brand, I went against traditional Chinese kung fu practices of the day and combined different styles to make my own.

Jeet Kune Do

This didn't sit well in the Chinese community. And I was ridiculed. They didn't believe I should be changing the traditional way of doing things or teaching martial arts to people who were not Chinese.

My philosophy was different. I loved it so much that I wanted to share it with the whole world. I believed everyone should have access to martial arts.

One day, I was asked to perform in a martial arts exhibit. While there, I demonstrated one of the techniques I learned under the YIP man - the one inch punch.

My performance was impressive enough to garner the attention of a television producer. And I was soon cast as Kato, in a supporting role, in a new show called *The Green Hornet*.

I wanted to pursue a movie career. To me, movies were a way to reach more people and spread my love of martial arts, even further.

But I found racial prejudice in Hollywood. At the time, they weren't interested in a Chinese leading man.

I was frustrated and living in near poverty with a family to support. So I decided to take a big risk.

I took my talents to Hong Kong.

After my success overseas, Hollywood came knocking and I made my first Hollywood Movie - *Enter the Dragon*. The movie was a box office hit! It went on to become one of the greatest martial arts films of all time. But maybe even more importantly, we helped bridge the gap between the *East* and the *West*.

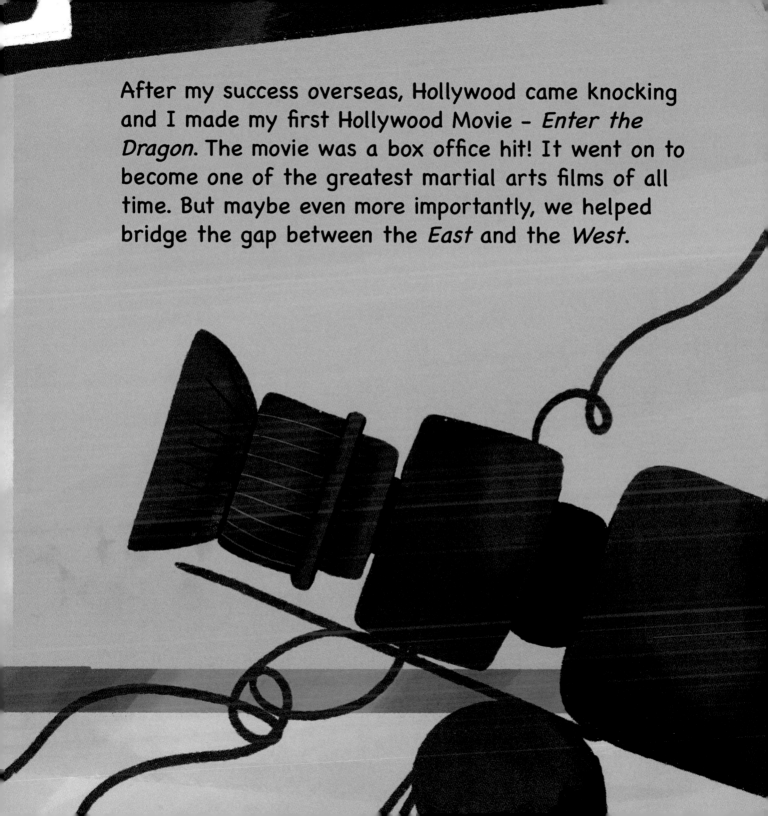

I had the courage to pursue my passions despite the risks and obstacles. And I was not afraid to be relentless in my pursuit of excellence.

racial prejudice

Poverty

Lost opportunities

You must be shapeless, formless, like water.

When you pour water in a cup, it becomes the cup.

When you pour water in a bottle, it becomes the bottle.

When you pour water in a teapot, it becomes the teapot.

Water can flow or it can crash. Become like water my friend.

Timeline

1940 - Bruce born in San Francisco

1958 - Bruce wins the Hong Kong Cha Cha Championship

1959 - Bruce moves back to America

1964 - Bruce gives a demonstration at the First
International Karate Tournament

1971 - Bruce films *The Big Boss*

1973 - Release of *Enter the Dragon*

1993 - Bruce receives a star on the Hollywood
Walk of Fame

1994 - Bruce is awarded the Hong Kong Film Award
for Lifetime Achievement

1999 - Bruce is named one of the most influential
people of the 20th century

2005 - A statue of Bruce is erected on the Avenue
of Stars in Hong Kong

minimovers.tv

 @marynhin   @GrowGrit
#minimoversandshakers

 Mary Nhin   Grow Grit

 Grow Grit

Made in the USA
Columbia, SC
22 September 2021